ANTIETAM ELEM. LIBRARY

P9-APF-296

I Love My Papi!

ANTIETAM ELEM. LIBRARY

by Alison Inches
illustrated by Dave Aikins

Ready-to-Read

Simon Spotlight/Nick Jr.

New York London Toronto Sydney

Based on the TV series *Dora the Explorer*® as seen on Nick Jr.®

SIMON SPOTLIGHT
An imprint of Simon & Schuster Children's Publishing Division
1230 Avenue of the Americas
New York, New York 10020
Copyright © 2004 Viacom International Inc.
All rights reserved. NICKELODEON, NICK JR., *Dora the Explorer,*
and all related titles, logos, and characters are registered trademarks of
Viacom International Inc.
All rights reserved, including the right of reproduction in whole or in part in any form.
READY-TO-READ, SIMON SPOTLIGHT, and colophon are
registered trademarks of Simon & Schuster.
Manufactured in the United States of America

10 9
Library of Congress Cataloging-in-Publication Data
Inches, Alison.
I love my Papi! / by Alison Inches ; illustrated by Dave Aikins.—1st ed.
p. cm. — (Ready-to-read)
"Based on the TV series Dora the Explorer as seen on Nick Jr."
Summary: Dora and her Papi play baseball, go to the beach, read books, and do lots of other fun things together.
ISBN-13: 978-0-689-86495-7 ISBN-10: 0-689-86495-7
[1. Fathers and daughters—Fiction.] I. Aikins, Dave, ill. II. Dora the explorer (Television program) III. Title. IV. Series.
PZ7.I355 Iae 2004
[E]—dc22
2003014360
0311 LAK

My PAPI and I love to do things together!

PAPI taught me a super
soccer kick. Look, I kicked
the SOCCER BALL into the GOAL!

We also love playing .

BASEBALL

PAPI coaches my team.

He taught us how to swing the  and slide into home  .

BAT

BASE

On weekends  and I

PAPI

ride  together.

BIKES

Or sail on a .

BOAT

Sometimes we go to the

together.

We build giant and

SAND CASTLES

play in the .

WAVES

My  is a really good  .

PAPI COOK

He taught me how to bake a special  and make yummy  .

CAKE

SANDWICHES

Sometimes we pack a 
PICNIC
and share it with my friend  .
BOOTS

My  made us this 

PAPI TIRE

swing! He can build

anything with  .

TOOLS

One time took us to
PAPI
the . loved the .
CIRCUS
BOOTS
CLOWNS

Then bought us and
PAPI
POPCORN
for a treat.
STRAWBERRY
ICE CREAM
Yum! Yum!

POP
CO

At the end of every day

PAPI

tucks me into  .

BED

Then we read a  .

BOOK

I like  about  .

BOOKS ANIMALS

says, "I love my !"
PAPI
DORA
And I say, "I love my !"
PAPI